Toby and the Nighttime

TOBY and
the NIGHTTIME

by PAUL HORGAN

illustrated by Lawrence Beall Smith

ARIEL BOOKS

Farrar, Straus and Company · New York

77132

To Chico with thanks for Chipper and Willie,

and to

F. A. O. Schwarz's, the open secret of this story

Toby and the Nighttime

Do you know that store—the biggest toy store in town?

It is on the corner of the Great Avenue and one of the busiest cross streets.

I used to go and stand there when I was your age and look in the windows, one by one. I stood there by the hour if they let me. I put my finger out and pressed it on the glass, pointing first at one toy, then another, thinking of what the toys made me think of. I am afraid my finger made a smudge on the glass.

Everything in the window was tiny, or sometimes small, or even pretty big. But, of course, nothing was ever as big as the real thing it was like.

It does not matter how big or small anything is—everything is as real as real to you, when you go to the toy store and look in the window.

But as you know, you have to do this in the daytime, or in the evening, because late at night, the lights go off automatically, and it is hard to see anything then if you can look through the window, and everything seems to go to sleep, and stay quiet, the rest of the night, until morning comes again.

I know about something amazing that happened at the store not very long ago.

It seems that the young man who was in charge of putting toys in the window for you to look at when you go by—his name was Mr. Herbert—it seems that Mr. Herbert picked out some specially wonderful toys a week or two ago and began to arrange them in a fine display. I remember what they were.

I remember a wonderful toy tug boat. It was fairly big—it would take both your arms to hold it. It was green on top, and red underneath, on the part which would be under the water, and it had a black hull and a black funnel.

4

I remember a beautiful yellow toy sports car. The car was much smaller than the tug boat. Two crash helmets with goggles were placed near it as though waiting for the driver and the mechanic.

I remember a toy freight train with a diesel engine and seven cars, all different colors.

I remember a toy atomic submarine with a Polaris missile, all black and wet-looking, like the skin of a whale.

And—this is the last thing—I remember a toy inter-planetary rocket. It was held upright in its gantry by steel scaffolding. It rested on a launching pad. On top of the rocket was the space capsule where the pilots would ride. Two space suits with helmets and face plates were arranged beside the rocket.

When he had placed all these things in the big window, Mr. Herbert decided he needed something to make them all look even more real than they looked already.

"I know," he said to himself, "I need a model of a little boy, looking as if he were playing with these toys."

He knew where to find his model. Upstairs in the stock room of the great store they kept all kinds of imitation people who could be put in the windows looking as if they were being interested in things. Mr. Herbert went upstairs.

The stock room was crowded with many piles of boxes,

and shelves, and imitation figures of all kinds of people. Some had clothes on and some didn't. Some even did not have arms or legs or heads. They were like big dolls that came apart.

Mr. Herbert wasn't looking for any of those.

He wanted to find an imitation figure of a boy which he called Toby, because it made him think of a real little boy he knew.

Toby was made all together, and did not come apart anywhere. No, Toby had elbows and knees, and Mr. Herbert could have him stand, or sit, or bend over, or turn sideways, like a real boy. But of course, once he was placed in the window, he did not move, the way a real boy can—or at least, that is what Mr. Herbert thought. Toby was as big as a boy six or eight years old, and very real looking.

His dark hair was trimmed close, like a real haircut, and his eyes were shiny and had real eyelashes, dark and thick, and his cheeks were tanned, but even so his freckles showed. He was dressed in a green pullover sweater, with a white shirt showing collar and cuffs, and a pair of gray corduroy trousers, and buckskin shoes with thick laces, and yellow socks. He had a referee's whistle on a white cord around his neck and from his belt he had hanging a flashlight with three colors of light bulbs—red, green, and white. And oh yes, on the back of his head he wore a small round cap of green felt, without any brim. When you looked at his cheerful face he made you feel cheerful too.

"Oh, there you are, Toby," said Mr. Herbert, coming around a pile of boxes and finding him. Toby was leaning against the wall looking up at the ceiling because of the way someone had leaned him. "Come along with me, young man," said Mr. Herbert. "I have work for you to do."

He picked Toby up and carried him under one arm as if he were a baby, which was not very proper, because Toby was no baby at all, but a make-believe little boy over six years old. They started through the piles of boxes in the stock room, heading for the elevators. All of a sudden a pile of boxes fell over in a tumble as they passed.

"Now who did that?" said Mr. Herbert, looking back.

And then he knew, for one of Toby's arms was fixed to stick out, and the way Mr. Herbert carried him, Toby could not help hitting the boxes with his hand, and the hand caught in one of the boxes, and the box moved, and when it moved, the whole pile fell over, and the top box fell open, and inside it was a toy dog.

He was a small brown and white dog, sitting down, with his head turned Toby's way. His red velvet tongue was hanging out, as if he were laughing—silently, of course, because he was a toy.

"Don't you laugh at me," said Mr. Herbert to the dog. "Look at this mess"—for there were boxes scattered everywhere.

Mr. Herbert turned Toby a little so his hand would not stick out and hit anything else.

8

"You did this, Toby," said Mr. Herbert. "You're just like a boy. Always into something. Now it's a brown and white dog. A dog," said Mr. Herbert, with pleased surprise in his voice, "a boy and a dog. I believe I'll use them both."

He leaned over and with his free hand picked up the little dog, who seemed to go perfectly with Toby.

"What's your name?" asked Mr. Herbert, looking the dog over carefully. But he soon had the answer, for the little brown and white dog with the laughing face had a collar, and on the collar, attached by a small round patch of squeezed tin, was a tag of stiff cloth, and on the cloth something was printed. It said,

"*Chipper.*" *Copyright.*

"All right, your name is Chipper. I don't care about the copyright part. From now on, you and Toby are going to work for me together."

Mr. Herbert took Toby and Chipper down to the big window on the sidewalk corner, and fixed them the way he wanted them to be with all the toys.

Toby was kneeling in the middle, and Chipper sat on the floor, looking up at him with his head cocked and his red velvet tongue sticking out. Toby's right hand was touching the tug boat, and his left hand was reaching for the rocket ship, and on the floor around him were the other toys—the sports car, the freight train and the atomic submarine.

Toby was looking at the air just above all the things. He looked something like—how shall I tell you? I know. Like this. You know how a young cat, or a big kitten, looks, when he is getting ready for something? That is how Toby looked. His eyes were wide open and still and bright, and he seemed to see something you or I could

not see. That is how a cat looks when he is busy. His pale eyes with the dark lashes are like two little lamps shining hard and bright. Toby was looking at things nobody else could see, not even Mr. Herbert, who put him there, with all his wonderful toys.

"Well, then, I guess that's it," said Mr. Herbert to himself, "I might as well go, until tomorrow morning."

The blue evening turned into a dark night. The avenue was misty. It wasn't raining, but it wasn't clear either. There seemed to be a fog coming over the city from the waterfront. Crowds went along the sidewalks, and the later it got the more they hurried.

But when they came to the store, and the corner window where Toby was kneeling with Chipper his dog and all his wonderful toys, most people slowed down, and looked in, and thought of how it felt to be a boy like Toby and to have such fine things to think about and such a charming little dog to be with.

Do you suppose that everything everybody felt about Toby—all the great thoughts they had about him—went through the big glass window and stayed there all about him in the air?

They knew he was an imitation of a small boy, but they felt real things about him.

They made him real by thinking about him.

12

He only needed the right time and the right chance to become real himself.

When do you suppose this might be?

I can tell you, for I know what happened at the store, when the lights went out, and everything seemed to go to sleep, by starlight.

Listen.

The lights in the window went out at half-past midnight. The street was almost empty. The fog was heavier —you could hardly see across the street. Inside the window all was dim and quiet, as though somebody was holding his breath and listening before making a move.

This seemed to last for a long time.

And then, softly, in a whisper, someone said,

"Chipper? Can you hear me?"

It was Toby speaking.

Because it was late at night, and nobody was looking, and everybody had made him feel so real, Toby was turning into a living boy.

The little dog wagged his tail. He was supposed to answer his master Toby. But can dogs speak? Who knows? Who was it who said, "Animals would speak if they had anything to say . . . ?" Somebody in France, wasn't it? No matter. Chipper now had something to say, since Toby had asked him something.

13

"Yes, Toby," he said, making words like little yelps, "I can hear you."

"Good," said Toby. "We have work to do. Come with me."

"Where are we going?" asked Chipper, panting so fast that his red velvet tongue turned pink.

"We're going to the river with our tugboat. Something is going on over there. Can you swim?"

"I don't know," said Chipper. "I never tried. Can you?"

"I don't know," said Toby. "Neither did I. Anyway, we may not have to swim."

"That's just as well," said the little dog, "since we are both made of cloth, and sawdust, and plaster, all of which would come apart in the water. What is going on at the river?"

"You will see in a few seconds. —There, already," said Toby. "See that, even in this fog?"

In the flash of an eye, the boy and his little dog, and their tugboat, were out of the great window in the big toy store, and were on the dark river that touched along the city on one side. Don't ask me how they got there— I do not know. All I know is that after midnight, when things have to be done, and nobody else is doing them, it may be that a toy boy and a toy dog and a toy tugboat can do them. Toby was the captain of the tug and Chipper was the crew, and the tugboat was all of a sudden so

14

big that it was just like a real one. They were going through the fog on the black water which was running fast with the tide.

"I see it," shouted Chipper, standing in the bow of the tugboat.

Ahead of them was a great enormous ocean steamer with all her lights out. Her engines were still. She made no sounds. She was out of control. She was drifting with the fast water in the river and if nobody would help her she would very soon smash to pieces alongside the rock and concrete edge of the waterfront.

Toby took his referee whistle and blew a long blast at the steamer.

"C-a-n y-o-u h-e-a-r m-e?" he called in a long voice, through the wind and the fog.

"Y-e-s," said a small voice from way up high on the great steamer, "but I can't see you."

Toby took his flashlight from his belt and switched it on, and made signals with it, first in red, then in green, and then in white light.

"Oh, now I can see you," they called from the big ship. "You are Captain Toby."

"Yes," said Toby. "I am here to save you. Catch this rope which my crew is just about to throw up to you."

"Thank you," they said from the ship, and then Toby, pushing and pulling his engine room controls, made the

15

tugboat go forward until he almost hit the ship, and then with his big pilot house wheel he made the tugboat turn and go sideways like a splendid duck, and then he made the tugboat come up right to the ship, and then he gave an order.

"Let go, crew!" he cried to Chipper.

Chipper looked around at him and said,

"You mean me?"

"Yes, you, you are the crew! Let go!"

"Oh," said Chipper, and then swinging *one, two, three,* with his great heavy rope over his head, he threw the rope coils up to the ship, where the sailors caught it, and tied it up on a large hook they had there for just such a purpose.

The night was dark, and cold, and foggy, and the hour was late.

There was not a moment to lose, or the great ocean steamer would go crashing against the city which stood over there in the fog, where the high buildings looked very dim, with their lights standing up in lines of golden dots.

"Here we go," called Toby, changing the engines of his tugboat. "I am going to pull you out in the river away from the shore, and stay with you until you can fix your lights and start your engines, and when you are running safely, I will let you go."

17

"How can we thank you?" they called from the ship.

"All I ask," said Toby, "is that you do not tell anybody about this. I am not supposed to be here."

"Very well, we will not," said the ship, "but you are a hero, and everyone should know it."

"No," said Toby, "my crew and I do this kind of thing because we are as real as real can be, but we do not want anybody to start doing it with us, and spoiling everything. Don't ever tell."

"We promise," said the ship.

The tugboat began to pull, *clum-chug, clum-chug, clum-chug,* way down deep in her engines, slowly pulling the enormous ocean steamer away from the waterside and out into the free part of the dark river.

Other tugboats and ships went by, and did not see Toby and his tugboat and his dog and his ocean steamer, but now and then they seemed to feel something, if they could not see it, in the fog, so late at night, on the cold, black, fast river, and they gave quick, sharp warnings with their horns or steam whistles, and once or twice they came close enough to have a smashup.

But nothing happened, and a few minutes before the first daylight began to show in the fog, when you could just see it by not looking at it straight on, all of a sudden all the lights came blazing bright from the ship. Her engines began to throb. The great ship was safe.

18

"We are safe now," they called from the ship.

"Good," said Toby. "It is just in time, for I was getting ready to leave you anyhow, because I have to be back at work before daybreak."

"Then we are most fortunate," said the ship. "We will now proceed under our own power, and all thanks to you, Captain Toby."

"You are welcome," said Toby. "Excuse me, please, if we go now. We have not much time."

"We will have to report this, you know," said the ocean steamer. "Everyone will want to know how we were saved in the middle of a breakdown, in the fog, on the black, cold, fast river, after midnight."

"Tell them anything you like," said Toby, "only do not mention me or my crew. Goodbye and good luck."

"Goodbye, goodbye," said the steamer, and then fainter, as Toby and Chipper and their tugboat drew away in the mist, and grew smaller and smaller, almost as small as toys, until they really were toys again, and finally vanished, "g-o-o-d-b-y-e. . . ."

The fog was almost all gone from the streets, and the daylight was growing on all the gray buildings, and looking in all the windows, when Toby and Chipper and their little tugboat appeared once again in their own window, and froze in perfect stillness among their wonderful toys, almost as if they had never been gone during the deep

19

hours of the night on the dangerous, black, cold, fast river.

Almost—but not quite.

For coming back in a hurry, they did not exactly remember the way they had been fixed there before, and someone who looked closely could see that everything was not quite the same.

For instance, Mr. Herbert.

He arrived at a few minutes before eight o'clock with the morning paper folded under his arm. Before he went to have his coffee at the corner drugstore, he wanted to see how his window looked today.

He looked, and then he looked again, and scowled. Something was wrong. He could swear that he left Toby the night before with his right hand touching the tugboat. But now Toby's right hand was resting on the little yellow sports car. And Chipper—Chipper was looking out at the street now instead of at Toby, the way Mr. Herbert had left him.

"How could it be!" snapped Mr. Herbert.

Nobody could have been in the window after him, for nobody else had the key to unlock the wooden wall behind the displays. He shook his head. Do you suppose some heavy trucks came by during the night and shook the street and the building and the toys and made everything jiggle into new positions? He slapped the newspaper with annoyance. Now he would have to go in the window and put Toby and Chipper back in the right positions.

But he had time to have his coffee, first.

At the drugstore, drinking his coffee—black, no sugar— Mr. Herbert read a remarkable story on the front page about an enormous ocean ship that had nearly come to a smash-up during the night, on the river, and was only saved by a mysterious tugboat, with a brave and clever captain, who had come out of the fog to the rescue.

"The captain and the crew," said the newspaper, "refused to be identified. The captain was quoted as saying

21

only, 'My crew and I do this kind of thing because we are as real as real can be.'"

Mr. Herbert thought this was a strange thing for the captain of a tugboat to say, and then went to the store, to put Toby and Chipper back in their proper places.

If he thought they were going to stay there forever, he was mistaken.

I am told there is only one place in the whole country where they have sports car racing all night long, by the light of the moon, and with more light along the whole course thrown by great high electric lights. The road for the races goes all over the side of a big mountain, up, and down, and around, and across, and up, and down, and around, and across, again and again. It is a very dangerous road with many turns and sharp curves. I am told there are many smashups.

One night the race started with fifty-seven cars. It would take them hours to run the whole race. There were red cars, and black cars, blue cars, green cars, purple cars, and everything but yellow cars.

No yellow cars.

That is what everyone thought, for when the race began there was no yellow car in the line-up.

But a little while after midnight, when the fifty-seven cars of all the other colors were racing all across and around that dangerous mountainside, everyone was amazed to see a yellow sports car with two riders in it suddenly appear on the road, and join the race.

The riders wore crash helmets and goggles, so you could not really tell who they were, but one of them was very much smaller than the other.

But I think you know who they were.

They were Toby and Chipper, and how they got there I cannot tell you, for I do not know.

All I know is that they had left the window in the big toy store and were now driving in a sports car race, for their toy sports car had now become as big as a real one.

Toby drove at first. He took the curves like a bird—you never saw such bright, sharp, safe curves as he took, but it looked, every time, as though he would have to smash up. People could not bear to watch him, but when he came to a curve they cried out,

"Look at that yellow sports car! Such wonderful driving! But so dangerous! I cannot bear to watch!"

But they could not help watching.

Toby and Chipper and the yellow sports car went so fast they passed all the other cars, not once, not twice, but three times.

"Why do we go around so many times?" asked Chipper, in a loud voice, because of the wind and the noise.

"We started late," said Toby, "and we have to catch

up with the others first for they have all gone around three times before we got here."

"Oh. I see," said Chipper.

"Here, Chipper," said Toby. "You drive for a while."

"You mean me?" said Chipper.

"Yes, you, you are my relief driver."

"Oh," said Chipper, and changed places with Toby while the yellow sports car kept right on going.

They came to a curve high up on the mountain.

The wind flew by them and their yellow sports car was like a bird, skimming the road and taking all the loops and turns.

Now at some of those turns there were loudspeakers which the racing officials used for announcements and such things.

As Toby and Chipper came roaring toward one of those loudspeakers, they heard the voice of an official say, very loud,

"Calling yellow sports car, calling yellow sports car!"

"Do they mean us?" asked Chipper.

"Yes. We are the only yellow sports car in this race," replied Toby.

"I wonder what they want," said Chipper.

The loud speaker told them.

"Calling yellow sports car," it roared, "what are you

24

doing in this race? You do not belong in this race. You did not start with the other cars. If you win you cannot have the prize because you did not enter properly. Leave the race course. Leave the race course."

"I wonder what the prize is?" said Chipper, driving superbly.

"It is probably a purse of eleventeen thousand dollars," said Toby.

"Should I drive off the course?"

"No," said Toby. "We will drive until we win the race, and then we will disappear just the way we came, and they can keep their prize."

"They can keep it," said Chipper. "What do we want with it?"

"I'll drive now," said Toby, and they changed places again. "I'm going to drive with one hand now, watch me."

He drove with one hand, and he leaned back on the leather cushions, and the yellow sports car went faster than ever, and everybody watching the race saw just a beautiful streak of yellow, moving like the wind over the whole side of the big mountain, up, and down, and around, and across. Toby passed car after car, not once, or twice, or three times, but four times, and the loudspeakers kept shouting out,

"Yellow sports car, yellow sports car, leave the race! Leave the race! You have already won it. You have set a new record, but as I told you, you may not have the prize on account of illegal entry."

"Illegal entry," said Chipper. "What does that mean?"

"It means we started after the others. Well, this car has had a nice little workout, and we have set a new record. We might as well go. It will soon be daylight."

"Yellow sports car, yellow sports car," cried the loudspeakers, "I warn you for the last time, leave the race or you will be arrested when you come to the finish line at the end of the last lap!"

But the yellow sports car never went to the finish line at the end of the last lap.

Nobody saw it go, or knew how it went, but all of a sudden, the yellow sports car, and the two drivers in crash helmets and goggles, were nowhere to be seen.

—Unless you happened to be downtown a little while later, and unless you happened to glance in at the big window of the store on the corner.

There was the yellow sports car, once again only as big as a toy, and there was Toby, and there was Chipper, all turned around again, but back at work in their window, waiting for everybody to come along all day and see them.

27

Mr. Herbert came along at the usual time and looked again at his window display. What he saw made him exclaim crossly.

"Look at that!" he said to himself. "It's all wrong again!"

For Toby and Chipper were not the way he had left them. Toby was leaning over to touch the toy freight train, and Chipper was lying on his side.

"What does happen to them during the night?" asked Mr. Herbert.

Well, you know, and I know, what happened to them during the night, but I don't think we would ever tell Mr. Herbert, and spoil their fun.

He went to have his morning coffee and when he read the paper, he read about a mysterious yellow sports car with two drivers, one much smaller than the other, in crash helmets and goggles, and how the yellow sports car, entering the race late, overtook and passed all other cars four times, setting a new record, and then disappeared leaving no trace.

But when he read this, Mr. Herbert never thought of Toby and Chipper and their car. They were just toys to him. After he had his coffee he went to the store and put Toby and Chipper back in their proper positions.

"I'm not going to let that Toby and that Chipper move around again," he said sternly.

As if he could stop them, after midnight was past, when the lights went off automatically, and the city was quiet, so quiet you could hear things that you never heard during the day, like ships on the river, or the engines of racing cars on a mountainside a long way away, or—listen! this is the next thing!—or the bell, and the horn, and the wheels, of a great freight train in the railroad yards at the edge of the city.

It was after midnight when the freight train started to move. It had seven cars, all different colors. In the diesel engine up front, the engineer was at the controls. He was a boy between six and eight years of age, with a round green cap on the back of his short-cut dark hair, and a strong look ahead in his eyes. It was—surely you have guessed—it was Toby, and his toy train was now as big and as real as any real freight train on the tracks leaving the city.

Next to him was Chipper, wearing a cloth cap with a long visor.

"You are the train conductor, Chipper," said Toby.

"You mean me?" asked Chipper.

"Yes, you," said Toby. "Take my flashlight and go back to all the freight cars and see what is in each car. We have many things to deliver before morning. Meanwhile I will stay here and drive the train. We are just entering the tunnel to go under the river. Be careful, but hurry. We must have everything delivered before daybreak."

"I will hurry and I will be careful," said Chipper. "We must not be late getting back, must we?"

"No, we must not," said Toby. "I don't know what would happen if we were not back in the store window by opening time."

"Mr. Herbert would be mad at us," said Chipper.

"Oh, I think something worse would happen than that. —Go along, now, conductor."

30

"Yes, sir," said Chipper, and began to climb back along the string of seven freight cars, all different colors.

The train entered the dark, cool, damp air of the tunnel. Toby watched for the signal light that would tell him when to go fast, with a great rush, into the darkness. He had his bright headlight shining, and when he got his signal, he pressed his controls, and the diesel engine, making a strong, fine sound like this—

gnnnnnnnnnnnnnnnnnnnnnnnnnnnnnnnnnnnnnnnnnnnnnnnnnn

which went higher as the train went faster, plunged down deep, deep, under the river, through the tunnel, and in a few minutes came out into the fresh night air on the other side of the river.

Everything was dark and quiet and late.

"Where is my train conductor?" asked Toby, and then he heard Chipper coming into the engineer's cab of the engine.

"Here I am."

"What have you to report, conductor?"

"I know what is in every one of our seven cars."

"Very well, what is in the last car?"

"The last car," said Chipper, "is filled with chocolate peppermints."

"Good," said Toby. "I happen to know they are all out of chocolate peppermints in Philadelphia. That will be our first stop. We will give them all our chocolate peppermints." A thought came to him. "Chipper," he said, "did you take so long because you stopped to eat some of those chocolate peppermints?"

"One or two," said Chipper.

"I thought so," said Toby. "Did you bring me one?"

"Yes," said Chipper. "Here"—and he handed a chocolate peppermint to Toby, who took it, ate it, and smacked his lips.

"That is a fine chocolate peppermint," said Toby. "They will love those in Philadelphia. We are almost there. Get ready to unhook the last car so they can unload it while we are off doing the rest of our errands tonight."

"Yes, sir," said Chipper. He went back to the last car, and when Toby stopped the train at Philadelphia, where many people stood by the tracks waiting for the chocolate peppermints he had brought them, Chipper uncoupled the car and gave Toby a signal with the flashlight, green—red—white—, which meant *All right, go ahead.*

"Oh, thank you, this is splendid," said all the people of Philadelphia, unloading the chocolate peppermints. "How can we ever repay you?" they said.

"Not at all," said Toby. "It is nothing. If people need something, I try to bring it to them. Goodnight, we have to go on, now."

The train, with six cars now, moved on in the dark night.

"What is in the next car, conductor?" asked Toby.

"I am not sure," said the conductor.

"Why not?"

"The car is loaded with a grillion little round plastic boxes, like pill boxes," said the conductor.

"Can you see inside the boxes?" asked Toby.

"Yes."

"Are there pills in them?"

"No," said the conductor, "just little pieces of paper."

"Oh," said Toby. "I know what *those* are."

"What are they, then?" asked Chipper.

"They are votes," said Toby. "That means we are going to Washington, where they always want votes."

He pressed the controls and the freight train flew faster along the tracks.

"Who are the votes for?" asked Chipper.

"The Congressmen," said Toby.

"How will they know which ones are for who?" asked Chipper.

"They will know which ones are theirs when they open the boxes and read the votes," said Toby.

34

The freight train went like the wind, and a few minutes later stopped at Washington, where the President and the Congressmen and a lot of other people, with a brass band, were waiting at the station for the votes.

Soon they had their carful, and the band played, and the President made a speech, and the train moved on to the next place.

There were five cars left now, and in the fifth car, there was a carload of fireflies.

"Let me see," said Toby. "Where did I hear they needed some fireflies? I know. Chicago. They are going to have a concert in the park and they want some fireflies to fly around over the grass and make it look magic, so little boys can chase after the fireflies. We will stop at Chicago next."

In a few minutes the train stopped at Chicago and Toby and Chipper left their car with its load of fireflies while the grown people and the small boys of Chicago thanked them with all their hearts.

The night was passing, and they had to hurry, and if they had to hurry, so must we, hearing about all of this, so we can get them back to their work before daybreak. They left a carload of baby chicks at Kansas City, where all the children planned to have a Happy Easter; and they left a carload of roller skates at Denver, where the boys and girls needed them to coast down the long slides

of the Rocky Mountains; and they left a carload of sugar at Salt Lake City, where it seemed that there was plenty of salt but no sugar; and last of all, they left a carload of gold and silver at San Francisco, where a long time ago—it was on television just yesterday—there was a lot of gold and silver, because people found it there in the rivers and in the earth, but after a while there was no more gold and silver, so they needed some now in San Francisco.

Now if you put your finger on the map as I used to do, and start at the Atlantic Ocean and go across the land until you reach the Pacific Ocean, you will know that Toby and Chipper, in their fast freight train, crossed the whole United States that night.

And then it was time for them to start back the way they came.

"We have finished our work for tonight," said Toby. "Now we must go back and pick up all our empty cars where we left them. And then we must go full speed back through the tunnel under the river, back to the city, and back to our window with our train, before daybreak. Are you ready, conductor?"

"I am," said Chipper.

"Here we go," said Toby, and the long, heavy diesel engine picked up speed, going all the way back across the whole United States, stopping for just a second at Salt Lake City, and Denver, and Kansas City, and Chicago, and Washington, and Philadelphia, to pick up the freight cars which they had dropped off to be unloaded at each place.

They went like the wind, for they were racing the night itself.

They were almost too late, for as they went flying along the railroad tracks toward the East Coast where the ocean was, and where the sun rose, they saw the darkness fall away behind them, like some great and beautiful black wing folding slowly away, and they saw ahead of them out of the engine cab the stars wink out and the first faint, pale light of day coming over the sea, as soon it would come over the land.

"Hurry," cried Chipper.

"Yes, more speed," cried Toby, and touched his controls, and the train went even faster, leaving Philadelphia, and coming to the tunnel. Once in the tunnel all was dark again, and it was like being safe again in the nighttime. From the tunnel to the store was only a little step, and by the time there was daylight in the streets between the buildings, Toby and Chipper and their freight train with seven cars, all different colors, were safely home from their trip across the United States and back. They were just toys again.

But they had returned in such a hurry that once again something was wrong with the way they sat in the window. The freight cars were piled up as though they had been in a wreck and Toby and Chipper were all sideways.

"What is happening to this country?" cried Mr. Herbert in a wild kind of voice when he saw conditions in the window. "All wrong again," he said. "And the things I

40

saw in the morning paper today during my bus ride! Nobody can explain any of it"—and he remembered what the paper said—how someone left a carload of peppermints at Philadelphia last night, and how someone left a grillion votes at Washington, and how in Chicago ten grillion fireflies suddenly appeared in the park. And that was not all, for the paper told how a hundred thousand baby chicks began walking all over Kansas City during the night, and then at Denver, how all the children suddenly had roller skates and were seen coasting down the slides of the Rocky Mountains. The paper told how a fast freight train with a diesel engine and different colored cars came into each town, and then left very fast, and how the next place it went was Salt Lake City, where the stores were filled with sugar, and finally, how gold and silver were discovered in San Francisco, just the way it used to be long ago.

Mr. Herbert went to work putting Toby and Chipper and the freight train back where they belonged, and said to himself,

"You would think that late at night, when everybody else is asleep, and nobody is watching, you, Toby, and your dog Chipper here, suddenly get up and go off to who knows where, and that when you come back, you are just too scatter-brained to remember the way you *should* sit here with your toys."

41

If Toby and Chipper heard what he was saying, they gave no sign; but you know, just as I know, that Mr. Herbert, without knowing it, was very close to their secret.

But he would never believe what you know and I know—even if we told him—about Toby and the nighttime.

We can be glad of this, for if he ever believed it, then he would try to think of ways to keep them from going out on their adventures after midnight, when nobody would be watching if an atomic submarine might be slipping down the river toward the bay, going fast and silently, with only its periscope showing a little way above the water.

It seemed to be very much like Toby's toy atomic submarine—and that is exactly what it was, as you have already decided, only it was now as big as a real submarine. You also know who her commander was—it was Toby.

He kept his eye to the periscope down inside the atomic submarine, watching to see that his ship, which looked like a great fish with a blunt head, did not hit the city beside the water, and he watched the radarscope to keep the ship away from the rocks below the water.

Chipper was at the engine controls.

"You are my submariner, Chipper," said Commander Toby.

42

"You mean me?" asked Chipper.

"Yes, you," said Toby. "It takes two of us to run this warship."

"Are we going to war, sir?" asked the submariner.

"No," said the commander, "even though we have a Polaris missile with an atomic warhead, which could blast anything, anywhere, *ksh-froo!*"

"What are we going to do then, sir?" asked the submariner.

"We are going out to the middle of the Atlantic Ocean to look for Willie the Talking Dolphin," said Toby.

"Who is he?" asked Chipper.

"He is a fine fish from Florida, where they have a marine zoo that is a zoo for fishes. He learned to talk just as well as we do, and he was the best thing in their marine zoo, because boys and girls came from all over the United States to talk to Willie, and ask him questions, and feed him peanut brittle, which he loves to eat."

"I am fond of it too," said Chipper.

"Yes, so am I," said Toby. "But I was talking about Willie. He worked hard, just like someone in a circus. He gave his show several times every day. But then they did something to hurt his feelings."

"What did they do?" asked Chipper.

"They brought in a lobster from Maine that could dance. His name was Gloppus, and they had *him* give a

43

show several times a day, too, and the boys and girls went to watch Gloppus, the Dancing Lobster, and feed him gum drops, which he loved to eat, and pretty soon there weren't many people to talk to Willie."

By now the atomic submarine was way out in the bay, leaving the United States behind very fast.

"What did Willie do, then?" asked Chipper.

"Well," said Toby, "he said he would never talk again, and then he simply jumped over the wall of the marine zoo at Florida one night and swam down to the very bottom of the ocean and just stayed there. He is there now, not saying anything."

"I feel sorry for Willie," said Chipper.

44

"So do I," said Toby. "But I think he is behaving rather childishly."

"In what way?" asked Chipper.

"Just because he is no longer the center of attraction, he goes off and sulks at the bottom of the ocean," said Toby.

"Yes, I see," said Chipper. "Well, what are you going to do?"

"We are going to try to persuade Willie to come back. Nobody else could go after him but us, for it takes an atomic submarine to go so far and so fast and so deep to the bottom of the ocean to talk to dolphin."

"I see," said Chipper.

"Did you bring any peanut brittle?" asked Toby.

"Oh, yes."

"Good," said Toby. "We'll need it."

By now the atomic submarine was at the very middle of the Atlantic Ocean, only on top of it, not under it, and the sea was very rough.

"We are about there," said Commander Toby. "Prepare to dive, submariner."

"Yes, sir."

"Dive!" commanded the commander.

Chipper pushed his engine controls and the atomic submarine turned nose down and went fast and perfect, like a diver, straight to the bottom of the ocean.

Down there it was darker than night.

"Submariner, turn on the underwater searchlight," said Toby, handing Chipper his three-color flashlight.

"Yes, sir," said Chipper.

Chipper shined the flashlight through the underwater picture window in the side of the submarine and flashed it back and forth. Suddenly he called out,

"There he is!"

There was Willie the Talking Dolphin. He was perfectly still in the water, looking in at them with his mouth shut, as though he would never talk again. He had little eyes that looked sad and a long wide nose like a scoop.

"Willie!" called Toby, over his two-way underwater intercom.

No answer.

"Willie! This is Commander Toby and Chipper the Submariner. We have come to talk to you."

No answer.

Toby gave Chipper an important look, and Chipper knew right away what he wanted. Then Toby looked back at Willie again and said,

"Willie, would you like some peanut brittle?"

Chipper held up the peanut brittle box and shook it invitingly near the window.

Willie still did not speak, but he did make a slow, complete turn in the water, and then came back to look again at the peanut brittle, but from a distance.

Toby said to Chipper, loud enough so Willie could hear him,

"My, that peanut brittle looks good, Chipper. I just believe I'll try some." Toby took a piece and bit it. "My, that's good. Won't you have some, Chipper?"

"I just believe I will," said Chipper, taking a piece and biting it. "My, that certainly is good peanut brittle, Toby," he said.

"Chipper," said Toby, loud enough so Willie could hear over the two-way underwater intercom, "I don't think people are so crazy about Gloppus the Dancing Lobster, back there at the marine zoo at Florida, do you?"

"No, I don't think they are, Toby," said Chipper.

"I think they go to watch him and feed him gum drops just because he is a novelty, now. Don't you?"

"I certainly do," said Chipper.

"It won't last, do you think?"

"No. It won't last."

Toby watched Willie out of the corner of his eye. Willie was slowly coming close to the underwater picture window, listening hard and staring hungrily at the peanut brittle.

48

But he still didn't say anything.

Toby said to Chipper,

"What they all really want, you know, is Willie the Talking Dolphin. Who cares if that old lobster from Maine can dance? Anybody can dance. Besides, he makes all that clatter with his claws and tail. Let him dance, is what I say, if he wants to, and who cares if people watch him? What they really want is to hear Willie talk. A talking fish—now that is *really* wonderful. I wish Willie would come back to Florida with us, don't you, Chipper?"

"I certainly do, Toby."

Willie was right outside the picture window now. He was opening and closing his mouth as if he were eating peanut brittle.

"Have we any more peanut brittle, Chipper?" asked Toby, loud enough for Willie to hear. "It is M'm'm Delicious—so fresh and crunchy, with all the golden goodness of choice molasses, and all the tangy richness of selected peanuts."

"Oh!" suddenly groaned Willie out loud, with his face right on the window glass only a little bit away from the peanut brittle.

"Why," said Toby, pretending to be surprised, "here is Willie. I had forgotten all about him. Won't you have some peanut brittle, Willie?"

"Oh, yes! Oh, yes, please!" cried Willie.

"Here then," said Toby, shaking the peanut brittle out through the underwater communication chamber. "Take all you like."

Willie was starved for peanut brittle, which is one thing they don't have at the bottom of the ocean, as a general thing. In a second it was all gone.

"Chipper," said Toby, "let's have another box."

"Oh, thank you, Toby," said Willie, forgetting not to talk. He even talked while chewing, which was bad manners.

"You're welcome, Willie," said Toby. "Now, let's go home together, shall we, Willie?"

"They don't want me," said Willie.

"Oh, yes they do."

"No, they just want that silly lobster, and that flopping around that he calls dancing," said Willie.

"I think you will find," said Toby, "that by the time you get home, they will all want you again. Come on, Willie, It is almost morning. We haven't much time."

Willie hesitated for a moment, and then said,

"All right, I'll go. But on one condition."

"What is that?" asked Toby.

"That they get rid of that lobster."

"No, Willie," said Toby kindly but firmly, "that is

50

childish. You can't have everybody be away all the time just because you don't like them."

"Well, then, part of the time?" asked Willie, turning one of his little eyes at Toby cleverly.

"Well, then, perhaps part of the time," said Toby.

"Very well," said Willie. "I'll go if they will have that lobster stay out of sight while I am giving my show. I don't care what he does other times. But when I am giving my show, he must not be around."

"That seems fair enough," said Toby. "I'll tell the marine zoo it has to be that way. Shall we go now?"

"Yes, Toby, and thank you," said Willie.

The atomic submarine aimed upwards and back toward Florida. The waves were still high on top of the ocean, and Willie seemed happy. Leading the atomic submarine, he flew through the air from wave to wave, and pretty soon Toby had his atomic submarine doing the same, and before you knew it, they were at Florida, where Willie went home to the marine zoo feeling better. Toby had a word with the zoo keeper, and then said to Chipper,

"We must go get home, too, and fast."

The atomic submarine went under the water at top speed back to the city.

"I must say, Toby," said Chipper, "you handled Willie

51

very well. It wasn't easy, was it?"

"No, it wasn't," said Toby. "But it is good of you to mention it. In fact, Chipper, you are a very fine friend, and I don't know what I would do without you."

"Well," said Chipper, "that is because I am a dog. Aren't you glad I am not a cat?"

"Well, to tell the truth, I am, because though I like cats, and I have known some very pretty cats, I don't seem to see a cat going through thick and thin with me, the way you have done. Do you think you could go through one more job with me?"

"Certainly," said Chipper. "What would that be?"

"Oh, don't you remember?"

"Remember? You never told me."

"No, but that last toy in our window—don't you remember what that is?"

"I have to think," said Chipper, hanging his red velvet tongue out and thinking hard.

"Well, there it is," said Toby, for all of a sudden they were back at the store, and the atomic submarine was small again, and Toby and Chipper were sitting there, but not the way Mr. Herbert had left them; for now they were looking at the only toy which they had not made real out in the world after midnight, when the streets are quiet, and the sky is dark and there seems to be no place better to go than up among the stars, in your dreams, or maybe even in something real, like an interplanetary rocket.

"Those two villains!" said Mr. Herbert when he saw Toby and Chipper in the morning, all turned around from the way he had left them. They were staring now at the interplanetary rocket standing upright in its gantry on its launching pad, with a capsule on top, for the pilots.

Mr. Herbert went to work fixing Toby and Chipper the way he wanted them to be, and all the while he kept thinking about what the newspaper said this morning.

"More mystery," he said, between his teeth, "last night, at Florida, at the marine zoo. When Willie the Talking Dolphin had been missing for days, he suddenly came back, escorted by an atomic submarine. Now he has signed a new contract with the marine zoo, and everybody is happy—except perhaps Gloppus the Dancing Lobster. I don't know, I'm sure," said Mr. Herbert. "It is all too much for me."

And then he said to Toby and Chipper, as if they could hear him,

"Now listen, you two—you stay right here, and no

more falling over and turning around, do you understand? You would think I had nothing else to do but come down here every morning and straighten you both up again!"

But you know and so do I that as long as they had things to do, and things to do them with, Toby and Chipper would not be stopped, and they had one more thing to do, after midnight, when the stars were so clear and the sky was so faraway and open, waiting for them.

There were great flaring lights all about the launching pad, and the interplanetary rocket, no longer a toy, but big as a real one, as high as a church, stood in its gantry. There were tubes and hoses attached to it and little curls of frozen bloxygen came out like steam from the cracks, making a long hissing sound that never stopped, and another sound that kept up, rather softly, like this—*chumf-groo, chumf-groo.*

Space engineers and maintenance crews were everywhere, hammering, testing, tightening things with wrenches, and looking at enormous watches that were hung around so all could see the hands clicking away the last seconds before launching. The sky was clear. Conditions were perfect. Suddenly everything went silent except the hissing sound, and the other sound, *chumf-groo, chumf-groo,* and then someone shouted,

55

"Here they come!"

Everyone turned to look through the bright lights in the dark blue night.

And here came Toby and Chipper, in their space suits, walking like giants, slowly and spread apart, because the space suits were so heavy. They had their space face plates already fastened, but you could see through the front of their helmets who they were.

A cheer went up.

Toby waved and Chipper waved, for they could hear everything inside their helmets with their transitor radios.

Then without waiting, just as if they were going to go for a ride in a jeep, they climbed up the steps of the gantry. An elevator took them to the top of the rocket, and there they stopped, turned and waved once more, and then entered the pilot's capsule on top, way up there, as high as the highest point of a church.

The night seemed darker up there because most of the lights were down below on the launching pad.

Next thing you knew, the gantry was unlocked from the rocket casing, and the big steel scaffolding was pulled slowly away by giant cranes.

The rocket was standing free now.

The big hands on the watches clicked off the seconds of the count-down—*nine-eight-seven*—and the television

cameras began to go, and the hissing of the bloxygen became louder, and—at *five-four*—the other noise, *chumf-
groo*, stopped, and—*three-two-one*—a voice said,

"Zero!"

And at once, there was a blast of air at the base of the
rocket, and then in a flash, a great thunder of fire under
the rocket went shooting downward against the launching
pad, and then, with everybody looking up and waving
and crying out, though nobody knew they made a sound,
the interplanetary rocket began to rise very slowly, just as
slowly as you would show with your hand, rising up, and
then getting faster, and then very much faster, with a
tremendous wind of fire and the scream of power, and
then all of a sudden, everything seemed to be so fast you
could hardly follow it with your eyes, and Toby and
Chipper were launched into space.

"That was a perfect take-off," said Toby. They were
past the earth's gravity now.

"It is just like being in a rocking chair at home," said
Chipper. He and Toby felt light as air.

"You are the co-pilot," said Toby.

"You mean me?" said Chipper.

"Yes, you. Now I will tell you what our mission is. Nobody else knows."

"Our mission?" said Chipper in surprise. "I thought we

58

were just going for a ride, and have to be back by daybreak."

"Oh, we do, we do, all right," said Toby. "But we have
something to do which man has never done before."

"Well, what?" asked Chipper.

"We are going to try to capture a live star and bring it
back out of space. No one has ever caught a star before.
That is what we are going to do up here. —Just look out,
there, co-pilot. What a remarkable sight."

They looked out the window of the capsule, and saw
the entire United States spread out way down below like
a map, and they could see the lights of New York, Philadelphia, Washington, Chicago, Kansas City, Salt Lake
City, and San Francisco, clearer than the lights on a
Christmas tree.

"Those are all the places we went in our freight train,"
said Chipper. "Do they know we are up here?"

"Oh no," said Toby. "We will not tell anybody we are
doing this. Nobody knows who we are. We are not out
after publicity."

"No, of course not," agreed the co-pilot.

"Now, co-pilot," said Toby, "you take over, and steer
the rocket where I tell you. I am going to the Forward
Observation Tube, to look for just the right star to
bring back. It must not be too big, and again, it must

not be too little. I want a sort of medium-sized star, but a very bright one. —There!" he cried. "Perhaps that is it, turn a little to the right, co-pilot. I think we have found our star!"

Chipper was so excited that he barked instead of speaking, and turned the great rocket a little to the right. The rocket was travelling at a speed of eleventy grillion miles per hour. She responded very well to the controls.

"Now, straight ahead!" called Toby from the Forward Observation Tube. "Hold it there and slow down about five grillion miles per hour and I will get the Star-Grappler Device ready. Wait till you see this star, co-pilot. It is a real beauty. So bright. So clear. People are going to love it."

They were so far out in space and in the midst of so many grillions of stars that you wonder how Toby could pick out one star and keep his eye on it and how Chipper could maneuver the interplanetary rocket so delicately to keep right in line with that one star.

"That's good," called Toby, "steady, now, we have to match the speed of the star exactly. The star is travelling very fast, but not as fast as we are. Take her a little slower, a little slower, steady, we're just about ready."

The star was just a few reaches in front of the rocket now and Toby suddenly called to the co-pilot,

"Co-pilot, turn on the De-gravity-Floater Device!"

Chipper reached for a lever marked "De-Gravity-Floater" and pulled it toward him.

Instantly the rocket and the star both began to drift in space. No more rushing forward. No more passing all the stars and planets in space.

"You see," explained Toby, "the De-Gravity-Floater Device brings the star we want right into our own Influence Zone and when we start to float, then the star floats too. In this way I am able to extend the Star-Grappler Device through the Forward Observation Tube, grasp the star, and bring it into the ship. Watch me do it now, co-pilot," said Toby.

Chipper watched with fascination while Toby, moving very slowly and carefully, inched his way into the Forward Observation Tube. His movements made the interplanetary space ship rock ever so lightly, like a row boat when you step carefully into it. The star, just outside the Forward Observation Tube, also rocked ever so slightly, keeping time with the space ship.

The light from the star was wonderful—pure white, clear, steady, and visible everywhere in space, but not so bright it hurt your eyes to look at it. You could look right at the star for hours and not be blinded. You could see everything better by its light. It made you feel you were seeing everything truly, perhaps for the first time in your life.

"Steady," said Toby, but he really said it to himself.

He eased the Star-Grappler Device gently forward out of the tube and as carefully as a boy picking up a firefly, or a baby chick, or a kitten, he took hold of the star with his Star-Grappler Device, which was something like a long pair of tongs, and drew it back into the Forward Observation Tube. The light from the star lighted up the interior of the pilot's capsule.

Toby held the tongs out toward Chipper.

"See," he cried, "we've got our star! It is the first one ever taken alive, with all its light!"

The star was just exactly the size of the stars you see at night in the sky when you look up from earth. It was as big as the head of a nail, but it looked much bigger, because its light made such a crown all around it.

"Hurray, hurray," said Chipper, wagging his tail inside his space suit as much as he could.

"Now I'll just put our star in this specially prepared case which I brought along," said Toby, opening a little box with very thick sides. "It is a star case made out of voroglinium. The star will be perfectly safe inside, for the material of which the case is made can absorb starlight safely."

He performed this delicate operation, and then said, "Very well, co-pilot, I will take the controls now."

"Yes, sir."

"Turn off the De-Gravity Floater Device, co-pilot," commanded Toby.

"Yes, sir."

Chipper pushed the lever and immediately the space ship resumed its interplanetary rate of speed.

"Do you see that over there?" suddenly asked Toby, pointing out of the window.

"Yes—why it is the moon!" cried Chipper.

"How lucky for us," said Toby. "We will take a turn around the moon before heading back."

"Have we time?" asked the co-pilot anxiously.

"It is a risk we will take, this time," said Toby. "Who knows when we will ever have a chance to take a turn around the moon again? Nobody has ever seen the other side of the moon before. I think we should look."

He touched the controls, and the space ship went as fast as your own thoughts, and the stars went by the window like fireflies, and the planets blazed and sparkled, and the moon, off to the left of the space ship, grew bigger and bigger, and Toby and Chipper could see the face of the man in the moon very clearly for the first time in their lives.

"Well, look at that!" said Toby. "Who does he look like?"

"It is someone I know," said Chipper, "but I can't quite—"

64

"It is just like Mr. Herbert," said Toby, "only without any glasses."

They both laughed out loud to see the man in the moon up close, and find out that he looked like Mr. Herbert.

"All right, now," said Toby, "here we go around to the other side of the moon where nobody has ever been before."

The great interplanetary rocket made a long, wide curve, as if you held your arm way out and then brought it slowly and steadily around again, and Toby and Chipper looked at the other side of the moon.

"Why, that's nothing," said Toby. "It looks just like the front, only without any face."

"I see some little smudges," said Chipper.

"Yes," said Toby, "I think those are the fuel dumps where they get the fuel to burn to make moonlight. They naturally would not have those on the front. The light comes out the front. They would keep the fuel in the back."

"I see."

"Well, that's done. Now we'd better be getting back. —Oh, co-pilot, look out there now. What is that?"

"Oh, Toby," said Chipper, "we are late. That is the sun. It is daybreak. Give it all the speed you have."

"I'll try, I'll try," said Toby. "But I don't know, I don't know."

"Know what?" asked Chipper anxiously.

"I don't know whether we will be there in time," said Toby.

But he pressed the controls, and both he and Chipper leaned forward, trying to make the great rocket ship go faster, faster, and she wheeled, and turned nose down, and headed straight for the earth. Faster than they could think a thought, or I could think a thought, or you either, the space ship burned through space into the atmosphere back toward the earth and the United States and home.

But this time they were too late.

There was full daylight in the streets and people were going along, and cars were moving, and buses were running, and store windows were showing, and Toby and Chipper were not yet back in their places.

Mr. Herbert came along the walk to look in, and when he saw that they were not there, he took a step backward and put his hand on his head and said to anybody who could hear him,

"This time they are not even there! How can I open up the store if everything is not just right—in fact, perfect—before the lights can go on, and the fans start blowing in the air conditioners, and the elevator motors begin running, and the background music starts playing, and the doors start opening, and the people start coming in?"

From this you can see how important Toby and Chipper were, if nothing could happen at the store until they were back in their places.

The people were already at the doors on the sidewalk in front of the store, waiting to come in.

And then, all of a sudden, Toby and Chipper, and the interplanetary rocket came through the air, and the closer they came, the smaller they became, until they were just the size of toys again, and nobody saw them pass through the air, and the glass, until they were once again in their places inside the window.

"Hurry," whispered Toby to Chipper. "Sit up beside me. They can't open the store until we are in our places. Mr. Herbert is looking for us now."

"I'm ready," said Chipper.

"I'm sorry," said Toby. "It was that trip around the moon that delayed us."

"I know," said Chipper.

"But I'm glad we saw it, aren't you?"

"Yes," said Chipper. "And I'm glad we caught that star. Where is it?"

"It is down at the city hall," said Toby. "I dropped it by parachute as we flew home. They will find the box of voroglinium, and they will open it, and they will find the star inside."

"And then?"

"And then they will know what it is, a live star, the first one ever brought back from space, and they will keep it."

"What will they do with it?"

"I'm not sure," said Toby. "But I think they will put it up so the light of the star will shine on everything. Then people will see things better, and then they will know more about what to do about things."

"Well, that is fine," said Chipper.

"Hush," said Toby suddenly, "I think I hear Mr. Herbert coming."

"Yes, he is coming."

"Let's pretend we have never been away from here," said Toby.

"Yes," said Chipper.

"Goodbye, Chipper," said Toby. "I think after this, with no other toys left to make real, our work in the nighttime is all over."

"Goodbye, Toby. I think so too," said Chipper. "Thank you, Toby. It was fun."

"Thank you, Chipper. You are a real friend."

And with that, they had to be quiet, and sit still, and hold their heads just right, and look at their toys without blinking, and stay just where they were, just the way Mr. Herbert had fixed them in the very beginning. They looked like toys, now, as if they had never been any-where, or done anything.

Mr. Herbert came to the window from inside the store.

"Well," he said to himself, "I have looked everywhere, and I did not find them. I'll look in the window just once more."

Mr. Herbert opened the door in back of the window, and there they were—Toby, and Chipper, and all the toys, just as they were supposed to be.

"They're back!" cried Mr. Herbert, "and for once, they are in the right positions! Open the store," he called in a loud voice.

In a moment the lights went on, and the fans started to blow in the air conditioners, and the elevator motors be-gan to run, and the background music started to play, and the doors started to open, and the people started to come in.

The store was open again, all because Toby and Chipper were back where they were supposed to be, and everything was perfect.

In a little while there was great excitement at the City Hall because when the Mayor came to work that morning he found a small box made of voroglinium, and when he opened it, inside he found a live star, the first one ever to come into the possession of mankind.

The light it gave showed everything so clear and true that people could see how things really were, and what to do about everything.

The Mayor said the star would be kept forever in the City Hall where everybody could come to see it, and see everything with its light.

Where did the star come from? asked everyone.

The Mayor said it must have come by rocket ship from outer space.

Who brought it?

Nobody knew, said the Mayor. But whoever did bring it was a hero.

By this time Toby and Chipper were both back in the stock room again, where they had come from, and their toys were all back again in glass cases in the main floor aisles.

But who knows when they might again become real, and go out again after midnight to do wonderful things that nobody, not even the newspapers, can explain?

Nobody ever knew what they had done all this time, except me, and I have not told anyone, except you, and you must not tell anyone else, except your own children, years from now, when you are all grown up, and ready to have them know how things are after midnight, in the lovely darkness, when everything is alive in a special way, and toys and children have their own world by starlight.